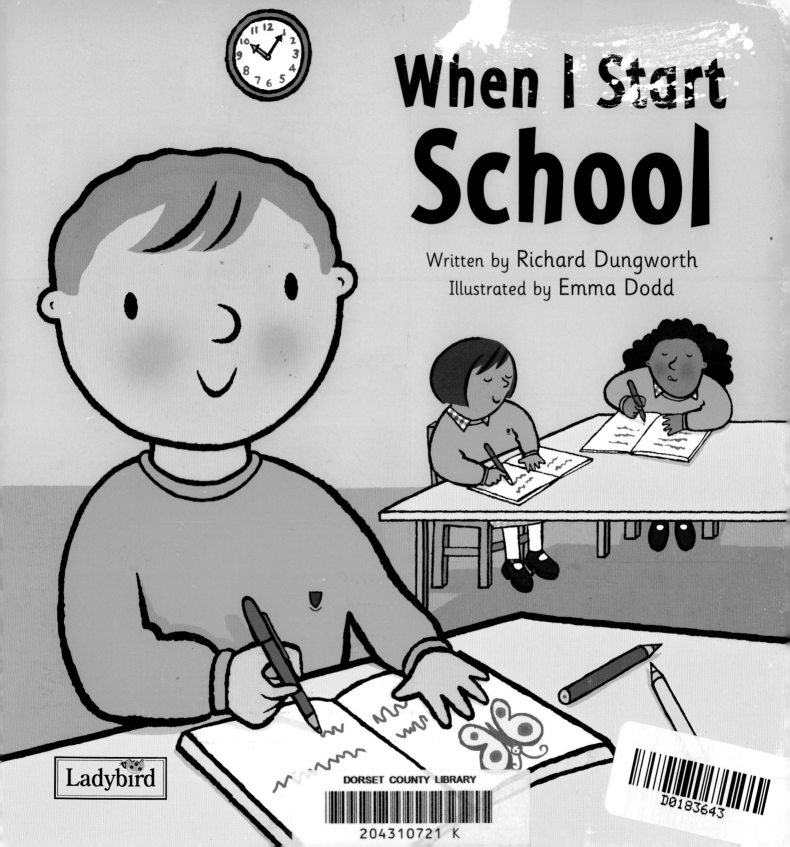

When I Start School

Written by Richard Dungworth
Illustrated by Emma Dodd

Ladybird

Tommy, Mummy and Sally are at the supermarket. Next week Mummy and Sally will come on their own because Tommy is starting school.

"Look, there's Robert, with his mummy! Give them a wave. You'll see him at school next week."

"Mummy, when I start school, how will I find my classroom? What if I get lost?

I don't want to get lost, Mummy. I don't think I'm ready for school."

"But you've been before for a visit, and you won't have to find your way around school on your own. I'll come into the class with you at first. After that Miss Sparks will help. You remember her, don't you?"

"Mummy, when I start school, I won't know anyone.
I won't have anyone to play with in the playground.

I don't want to be left on my own, Mummy.
I don't think I'm ready for school."

"But you won't be on your own! Robert's going to be in Miss Sparks' class, so you're bound to see him.

And there'll be lots of new people to be friends with."

"Mummy, when I start school, will I have to use a big knife and fork? Will I still have to eat my lunch if I don't like it?

I don't want to eat things I don't like, Mummy. I don't think I'm ready for school."

"But the food at your school is delicious! Maureen the school cook won a prize for her treacle pudding last year."

"Mummy, when I start school, what will I do if I need a wee?
I can't get on the toilet without my step-stool.
If I shut the door I might get stuck.

I don't want to get shut in the toilet, Mummy.
I don't think I'm ready for school."

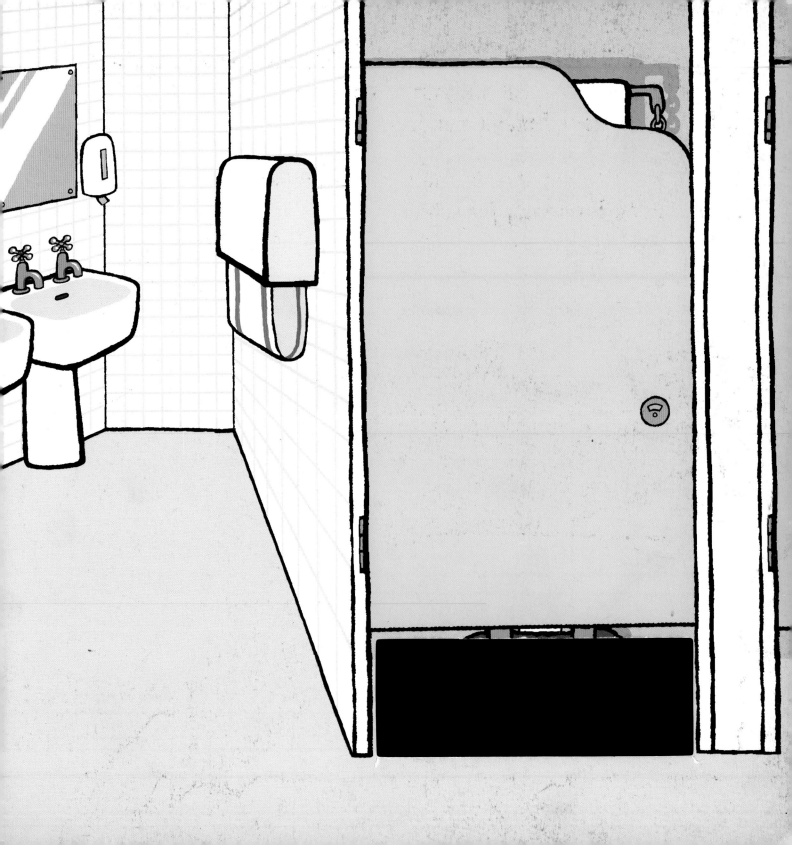

"But going to the toilet at school will be much more fun than it ever is at home! They have extra-special small toilets, just right for girls and boys. And you don't ever have to lock the door — you can leave it open. And you can do your own flushes."

"Mummy, when I start school, who will help you look after Sally?
And what about Bear? Who will he play with?

I don't want you and Sally and Bear to be left alone.
I'd better not go to school, Mummy."

"But Sally, Bear and I will be fine.
We'll miss you lots, of course, but we'll be busy
making something to show you or learning a
new game for when you get home."

"All right Mummy – if you're sure that you and Sally
will be okay without me...
and if Robert's in my class ...
and if we might have treacle pudding...
and if I can really flush my own toilet...

maybe I am ready to go to school, after all.

It sounds like fun."